A Note from PJ Library®

"Sukkot," explains Saralee, is "all about celebrating the harvest and welcoming guests." What could be more appropriate for a family of restaurateurs? The value of *hachnasat orchim* (Hebrew for "welcoming guests") is at the center of this weeklong holiday. A *sukkah*, the traditional temporary hut that families spend time in during Sukkot, makes it easy to welcome guests—even an entire town, as Saralee's family does in this story! What a wonderful way to observe a holiday that celebrates abundance, gratitude, and starlit cuisine. To learn more, visit pjlibrary.org/starlightsoup.

Sukkot arrives each year sometime between mid-September and mid-October. In Israel, it's often warm, but in other parts of the world it can be pretty chilly. A sukkah like the one Saralee's family builds is meant to remind us of the time when the Israelites wandered the desert after escaping slavery in Egypt. For the entire week of Sukkot, it's traditional to eat, socialize, and even sleep in a sukkah. And what if it's chilly? Break out the blankets, bundle up, and serve something hot and steamy! Starlight Soup, anyone?

A Note from PJ Library®

The flavor of Starlight Soup morphs depending on the taster. According to the Torah (the first five books of the Bible), when the Israelites were wandering in the desert, they ate manna from heaven. It's been said that manna tasted like one's favorite food, too!

Talk It Over

- When Harold suggests a joint Sukkot party, Saralee refuses. Why?

- How can you tell Saralee and Harold are good friends?

- What would Starlight Soup taste like to you?

About PJ Library

The gift of PJ Library is made possible by thousands of generous supporters, your Jewish community, the PJ Library Alliance, and the Harold Grinspoon Foundation. PJ Library shares Jewish culture and values through quality children's books that reflect the diversity of Jewish customs and practice. To learn more about the program and ways to connect to local activities, visit pjlibrary.org.

A SARALEE SIEGEL BOOK

Starlight Soup

A Sukkot Story

By Elana Rubinstein

Illustrated by Jennifer Naalchigar

For Ben—my SOUPer husband
— E. R.

For Hiro
— J. N.

Apples & Honey Press
An imprint of Behrman House
Millburn, New Jersey 07041
www.applesandhoneypress.com

Text copyright © 2021 by Elana Rubinstein
Illustrations copyright © 2021 by Behrman House

ISBN 978-1-68115-564-7

Library of Congress Cataloging-in-Publication Data

Names: Rubinstein, Elana, author. | Naalchigar, Jennifer, illustrator.
Title: Starlight soup : a Sukkot story / by Elana Rubinstein ;
illustrated by Jennifer Naalchigar.
Description: Millburn, New Jersey : Apples & Honey Press, [2021] | "A
Saralee Siegel book." | Audience: Ages 8-10. | Audience: Grades 4-6. |
Summary: Ten-year-old Saralee Siegel accidentally creates a magical soup
for the Jewish holiday of Sukkot and must use her heightened sense of
smell to save the town from a culinary disaster.
Identifiers: LCCN 2020038298 | ISBN 9781681155647 (hardcover)
Subjects: CYAC: Smell--Fiction. | Sukkot--Fiction. | Restaurants--Fiction.
| Jews--United States--Fiction.
Classification: LCC PZ7.1.R8276 St 2021 | DDC [Fic]--dc23
LC record available at https://lccn.loc.gov/2020038298

Design by NeuStudio
Edited by Dena Neusner
Printed in the United States of America

1 3 5 7 9 8 6 4 2

0921/B1738/A8

Contents

Chapter One
The Etrog Game

I've seen some wacky noses in my ten years of life.

Seriously, I've seen squishy noses and crooked noses. I've seen pointy noses and pancake noses. I've seen lumpy noses, and bumpy noses, and even short, stumpy noses.

But this I know for sure. No one in the world has a nose quite like mine.

"All righty, Saralee," said my grandfather, Zadie. "Get your sniffer ready. On your mark, get set, GO!"

I zipped up my jacket and dashed out the door. I only had fifteen minutes to finish the game, and I needed every second of it.

Outside, I took a deep sniff with my super-nose.

Where was that etrog?

An etrog is a yellow fruit that smells like pure sunshine. One little sniff and I'm transported to an easy, breezy afternoon with clear skies.

We smell the etrog during the Jewish holiday of Sukkot. The day before the holiday begins, Zadie and I play this made-up game. He hides the etrog somewhere around town, and I use my nose to find it. Literally, the etrog could be any-where—the schoolyard, town hall, you name it!

I squeezed my eyes shut, trying to concentrate.

Sometimes, I like to imagine that there's a flavor laboratory inside my nostrils. There are little nose scientists bustling around, writing down all the different smells. They sniff a little bit here, a little bit there until . . .

"Aha!" I cried out loud. "Gotcha."

I could smell the etrog clearly now. All I had to do was follow the trail.

Fast as I could, I sprinted past the barbershop, the shoe store, and the park. I ran until the etrog scent grew stronger than ever. My super-nose tingled, and I stopped in my tracks.

I stood directly in front of the grocery store.

Interesting choice, I thought. *Zadie hid the etrog here?*

But I had no time to doubt myself. I hurried inside and instantly knew where to go. My nose led me through the cereal aisle, past the display of salad dressings, and straight to the fruit section. I stopped in front of the lemon display.

Wait. . . . Lemons?

Uh-oh.

I gulped and looked at the pile of yellow fruits. Had my nose been confused? Had I followed a lemon scent instead of an etrog smell?

The two fruits smelled so similar. . . .

I put my hands on my hips and took another

deep smell. No . . . I definitely smelled something sunny, something easy and breezy.

I definitely smelled an etrog.

Carefully, I hunted through the pile of lemons. I searched, and sifted, and scoured until I reached the bottom of the pile.

Then I smiled.

At the very back of the lemon display was the beautiful etrog. I held it up to my nose, breathing in its refreshing scent.

Ha-ha! I thought. *Super-nose for the win.*

As you probably can tell, my nose is my secret

weapon. I can sniff out ingredients like no one's business.

Suddenly, someone tapped me on the shoulder.

"Time's a-ticking," said Mr. Green, the shopkeeper. "You'd better hurry."

Without thinking twice, I streaked out the door. The sun was already beginning to set.

I couldn't wait to show Zadie the etrog.

Thanks to my super-nose, I'd won the game!

Chapter Two
Menu Mission

"Thirteen minutes and twenty-nine seconds," said Zadie.

He stood in the middle of the sukkah, smiling from ear to ear. Tonight, he wore an apron with a jacket on top. His hair glowed silver in the evening light.

I love my grandfather so much. He's the best chef in the whole world, and he always smells the same: like peppermint with a hint of corned beef on rye.

My zadie runs our family restaurant, Siegel House. The two of us make the perfect team. He's a master chef, and I'm a master sniffer. Together, we're like two peas in a pod.

"Hey! You almost tricked me," I said, laughing. "You hid the etrog under a pile of lemons."

Zadie squeezed my cheeks. "If you think *that* was hard—just wait till you see my hiding spot next year."

I smiled.

Sukkot is an amazing holiday at Siegel House Restaurant. It's a Jewish holiday all about celebrating the harvest and welcoming guests. Of course, that's no problem for my family. We're experts at sharing delicious food with others!

Zadie likes to say that every guest brings a little more Sukkot joy. That's why we try to have as many guests as possible during the holiday.

My family builds a huge sukkah on the back patio. A sukkah's like an outdoor house with no roof (it's covered with branches and leaves instead). And for a whole week our guests sniff the etrog and dine in the great outdoors.

I watched as Zadie put the etrog away in its fancy box.

"Now, Saralee," he said, getting all serious. "Are you ready for business? I have an important mission for you."

A mission?

I love a good mission—especially if it involves sniffing desserts.

"What do you need?" I asked.

Zadie cleared his throat. "Well, the thing is, I've been cooking and cooking all afternoon. And I hate to say it but . . . I think I'm *bored* with the menu."

I squished my eyebrows together. "Bored? You can't be serious."

Zadie always makes the best food for Sukkot. There's crunchy pomegranate salad, autumn vegetable stew, smoked brisket, stuffed cabbage, garlic roasted cauliflower, and cherry crisp for dessert.

Zadie frowned.

"We keep making the same Sukkot recipes over and over. I want to give our guests something fresh. Something that's never been done before."

Zadie reached out and bonked my nose. "Got any ideas in that schnoz of yours?"

I gave him a wicked smile.

Ideas? Me?

Of course I have ideas.

Not to brag or anything, but I'm like an encyclopedia of scents and flavors. I can create a brand-new recipe in nothing flat.

I needed some inspiration, though.

"Well, what's your favorite part of the holiday?" I asked.

Immediately, Zadie tilted his head back, looking through the roof of the sukkah. "The view, of course."

I followed his gaze.

On Sukkot, you're supposed to see the stars between the gaps in the branches. Tonight, the stars twinkled brightly. They were like perfect

glowing candles, lighting up the night sky.

Huh, I thought. *The stars* . . .

Suddenly, my super-nose got all tingly.

An idea began to form in my mind.

What if the stars had a *smell*? What if they had a flavor?

I could make starlight salad . . .

Or starlight spaghetti . . .

I gasped.

No, no, no—I had the perfect idea.

"Hey, Zadie," I said. "How do you feel about Starlight Soup?"

Chapter Three
The Smell of Starlight

"Starlight Soup . . . ," Zadie said. "Now *that's* an idea."

He put his arm around my shoulder. "So how do you make it, glow-in-the-dark broth?"

I shook my head. "No, Zadie. *Real* Starlight Soup. You know, with *real* star flavoring."

Zadie opened his mouth.

Then he closed it again.

"Star flavoring?"

I nodded. "Yes, of course."

I could just imagine it now—everyone dipping their spoons into a glowing bowl of pure light.

"Do you know how to find this . . . this star flavoring?" Zadie asked.

I nodded again, pointing to my super-nose. "Easy peasy lemon squeezy. All I have to do is smell my way to the stars."

Zadie took a deep breath. "Well—it's definitely fresh. It's definitely never been done before. I just . . ."

"What?"

Zadie paused for a minute.

"Come on, Zadie," I prompted. "I *know* I can do it. This is my super-nose we're talking about. When has it ever let you down?"

Zadie looked at me with his big, brown eyes. And then, slowly, his face split into a smile.

"You know what," he said. "What's the harm? Go ahead and give it a try. You think you can make it soon? Sukkot starts tomorrow evening."

I nodded.

"I'll sleep in the sukkah tonight," I said. "I bet I can make Starlight Soup before sunrise."

That night, my little cousin, Josh, and I set up sleeping bags in the sukkah. Outside, everything looked dark and unfamiliar. But our sukkah felt all cozy, like eating a warm pumpkin pie on a freezing night.

Josh snuggled in his sleeping bag and closed his eyes.

"Wait, don't fall asleep," I said. "We have a very important mission tonight."

Josh is only in kindergarten. He thinks he's a real doctor and never goes anywhere without his toy doctor's bag.

"Wha . . . what is it?" he mumbled, opening one eye. "Do you need a Band-Aid?"

"No. Josh, wake up—"

He rubbed his eyes. "I'm sleepy, Saralee."

"I know," I whispered. "But tonight we're

making *Starlight Soup*. We're going to bring the light of the stars into our sukkah . . . and it's going to be amazing!"

"You sound like a crazy person," Josh yawned.

I grabbed a soup pot from the outdoor kitchen and filled it up with water. All I had to do was sniff out some star flavoring from outer space.

"I need to use your doctor's bag," I said.

Josh sat up and bit his lip. Then he gave me a look.

"I promise I'll be careful with it," I said. "I just need to use the Ace bandage."

Slowly, Josh slid his doctor's bag toward me. "Can you put it near my pillow when you're done? I need it to sleep good."

Before I could answer, Josh covered himself in a mountain of blankets. He was fast asleep a moment later.

The night suddenly felt very quiet. I shivered.

An owl hooted somewhere in the distance. The lantern made shadows on the sukkah's walls.

Quietly, I opened Josh's doctor's bag and went digging for an Ace bandage. When I cover my eyes and ears, my super-nose gets unbelievably strong. I call this going into over-smell.

I tied the bandage around my head, and the entire world was suddenly one giant mess of smells and scents. I could smell Zadie's late-night coffee. I could smell the roses growing in front of town hall. And someone somewhere was hosting a bonfire, complete with hot cocoa and marshmallow s'mores.

But nothing smelled like starlight.

Nothing at all.

So I pushed my nose harder. I imagined floating up into the night sky. I could smell the fresh, sharp air. I could smell the sweet cotton-candy clouds. I kept sniffing higher and higher until I got goose bumps all over my body.

And then . . . I did something incredible.

I stretched my nose as high as it could go.

I pushed my nostrils harder than ever. And before I knew it, I was smelling space. Real-life SPACE!

There was no air out there. Just the smell of smoke and ashes. The sun smelled like hot metal. I passed space rocks and asteroids, and the moon, which smelled just like dust.

I smelled my way through the universe until I finally reached the stars.

The amazing, dazzling stars.

I took a deep breath . . . and *there*.

I found the smell I needed. After sniffing for trillions of miles, I'd actually found the smell of starlight.

Chapter Four
An Impossible Taste

I'm not even sure how to explain this. I smelled something indescribable, something *magical*.

The starlight smelled like all of my favorite scents combined into one. It was Zadie's cheese blintzes and sweet potato pancakes. It was double chocolate-chunk cookies and kosher dill pickles. It was every single one of my favorite foods all tangled together.

I breathed it in until my nose was bursting with the smell of starlight. I imagined the star flavor traveling down from space and zooming into my soup pot.

That's when something strange began to happen.

The air around me grew warm. Was that steam? The air grew warmer and warmer until it was hot, hot, HOT. I backed up a few steps.

Carefully, I lifted the bandage from my eyes.

The water in the pot was glowing. It filled the sukkah with golden light. When I looked down into the liquid, I could see a million little stars twinkling brightly.

"Holy moly guacamole," I whispered. "It actually worked."

Thanks to my super-nose, I had captured the flavor of starlight in the pot. This was real. Starlight Soup was real!

"Josh," I squealed. "Joshy, wake up. You won't believe what happened."

Josh cracked one eye open, then the other. Then he saw the glowing soup pot on the ground. He jolted awake.

"Oh wow," he breathed. "Gimme my doctor's bag."

I handed it to him so he could examine the soup. He studied it with his magnifying glass and took the temperature with his thermometer.

"Let's try it," I said.

I grabbed two spoons from the outdoor kitchen.

"Is it safe?" Josh asked. "Remember when I

nibbled my science project?"

I rolled my eyes. "You ate glue, Josh. This is different."

"But Saralee—"

"Come on, what could go wrong?"

Josh hesitantly took one of the spoons.

"Okay, on the count of three," I said.

"One . . ."

"Two . . ."

"Three."

We plunged our spoons into the golden liquid. And immediately, I knew my life was changed forever.

I tasted the exact flavor of my favorite soup— Golden Carrot. I could taste all the ingredients: carrots, leek, fresh ginger, creamy coconut milk, crisp apples *and* apple cider, veggie stock, honey, turmeric, a dash of cinnamon, and a sprinkling of salt. It was perfect.

I closed my eyes and savored the taste.

Golden Carrot Soup is really special to me. Once, when I was three years old, Zadie made a big pot of Golden Carrot Soup for dinner.

Apparently, I took one sniff and then listed every single ingredient down to a pinch of salt.

It was a famous day in Siegel House history. It was the day we discovered my super-nose. How funny that Starlight Soup tasted like this *exact* recipe.

"Crazy!" I yelled.

"Yummy," cried Josh. "It tastes just like Zadie's chicken soup."

I cocked my head to the side.

"You don't taste Golden Carrot Soup?" I asked.

Josh shook his head. "No, it's definitely chicken soup with extra noodles. You know, the one Zadie makes when I'm sick."

My mouth fell open.

Could it be . . .

I thought about my nose traveling through the universe. Starlight had smelled like all my favorite flavors combined into one. So maybe Starlight *Soup* tasted like everybody's favorite *soup* flavor?

"Whoa . . . ," I started. "We have to wake everybody up RIGHT NOW."

Chapter Five
Out in Space

Ten minutes later, my entire family crowded around us in the sukkah.

"This better be important," huffed my aunt Lotte. "I can't believe you woke me up like that. You scared the living daylights out of —"

She looked down at the glowing pot. Her hand flew to her chest. "What in the world?"

Uncle Sam stood rooted to the spot. Tonight he wore his zip-up onesie pajamas. He clutched his favorite midnight snack (a cup of peanut butter chocolate pudding) in his hands.

"This is . . . this is incredible," he breathed, squeezing the pudding cup a little too tightly.

The gloopy chocolate plopped to the ground. *SPLAT.*

Normally, my aunt Bean would hurry to clean up the mess—but she didn't move a muscle. She just stared at the Starlight Soup, her eyes all wide.

"I'd like to introduce you to our new Sukkot dish," I said. "Starlight Soup!"

My grandmother, who I call Bubbie, looked around the glimmering sukkah. Starlight radiated from the soup pot.

"Space!" she cried. "We're floating out in space."

Bubbie is sometimes a bit mixed-up about things. She wears nightgowns like fancy dresses and also likes to make jewelry out of dried noodles.

I turned around to look at Zadie.

He was standing very still. He kept looking at the pot and then back up at the sky.

"Amazing," he murmured. "Simply amazing. I didn't think it would . . . golly, is it *real* star flavoring?"

I nodded. "Straight from outer space."

"Can we try it?" Zadie asked.

I handed out some spoons. If I was right, each one of my relatives would taste their favorite soup flavor.

Aunt Bean put on some hand sanitizer and wiped down the edge of the pot.

She took a dainty sip with her spoon. "Split pea . . . creamy and delicious."

"No, it's not," said Uncle Sam, taking a huge spoonful and spilling half of it on himself. "It's . . . it's beef and barley. Light on the barley, heavy on the beef."

Aunt Lotte rolled her eyes. "You guys are crazy. This is taco soup with sour cream and crispy chips. How can you not taste it?"

"By golly, Pookie Wookie—it's extra-noodle minestrone." Bubbie smiled.

Bubbie isn't so great with names, so she just calls *everyone* "Pookie Wookie."

I looked over at Zadie.

"What do you taste?" I asked him.

Zadie rubbed his chin. "My grandmother's famous mushroom and potato soup. It's . . . I haven't tasted this in years. It's perfect, just the way she used to make it when I was a boy."

His eyes suddenly got all watery.

"Excuse me for a second," he said. "I need a tissue."

I jumped up and down. "See! Isn't this incredible? Starlight Soup tastes exactly like each person's favorite soup flavor."

"So the soup tastes different to each of us . . . ," gasped Uncle Sam. He started pacing around the sukkah excitedly. He walked so quickly, he stubbed his toe on one of the chairs.

"Ouch," he muttered, hopping up and down.

The rest of my family began talking a mile a minute.

Only Zadie stood completely silent. I watched as he dabbed his eyes and looked up at the stars.

The soup brought the starlight directly into the sukkah. A little piece of the universe, right here in our backyard.

"Everything okay?" I asked him.

Zadie nodded. His eyes were sparkly as he looked at the glimmering pot of Starlight Soup.

"Mission accomplished, Saralee," he whispered. "By golly, mission accomplished."

Chapter Six
Pickled Herring

When I woke the next morning, I could still taste Starlight Soup on my tongue. I rubbed my eyes, snuggling deeper into my sleeping bag.

Had I *really* made a magical soup? Or was the whole thing just a dream?

I looked up through the roof of the sukkah. The sun was rising in the tangerine sky. I could hear the birds chirping softly in the trees. And the chilly breeze tickled my nose.

"Hey, Saralee," whispered Josh. "Are you awake?"

I rolled over so I could see him. He was wrapped up like a burrito in his blankets.

"I'm awake," I whispered back.

Josh grinned at me. "I can still taste it. I can still taste the Starlight Soup."

For a moment, my heart felt all fluffy—like a batch of homemade whipped cream. Thank goodness it wasn't a dream.

Starlight Soup was real!

At school that day, I couldn't wait to tell everyone the news. I sat with my class in the cafeteria during lunch.

"You will not believe what I made last night!" I said, opening my lunch box.

Today, I'd packed the Super Siegel Cheese Sandwich. It's the biggest sandwich on our restaurant menu. It has two slices of home-made bread, a hunk of mozzarella cheese, bean sprouts, two freshly cut tomatoes, and a ton of pesto.

The whole thing is bigger than my face.

"What?" asked Jacob Brodsky.

"A *magic* soup for Sukkot." I smiled. "The best-est, most magical Sukkot soup in all of existence."

Rachel Rubin twirled her hair around and around.

"Nuh-uh," she said. "Not *for-real* magic."

I smiled again. "Oh, it's for-real magic. Trust me."

I licked my lips. The magic was *so* strong, in fact, I could still taste the flavor on my tongue.

"Well, what does it do?" asked my friend Harold Horowitz.

Harold has bright red hair gelled into a spike on the top of his head. He has a mouth full of braces, and he always wears a tie to school.

"It's called Starlight Soup," I explained. "It tastes like everyone's favorite soup recipe. And it glows like real starlight."

Everyone just stared.

"You're lying," said Rachel. "That sounds impossible."

I gave her a wicked grin. "Come to Siegel House tonight. Then you'll see."

Everyone in my class started babbling about Starlight Soup. Well . . . everyone *except* for Harold.

See, Harold and his family own the other restaurant in town—Perfection on a Platter. Perfection on a Platter opened just a while ago.

And honestly, it's been a little complicated having a second restaurant around here.

At school, Harold and I are friends. But sometimes things can get weird, especially around a holiday. That's when our restaurants compete for sales the most.

Harold turned to me.

"Speaking of Sukkot," he said. "You're not the only one to have an amazing new idea. I thought of something last night—and I think it's gonna bring in a LOT of Sukkot guests."

"Oh yeah?" I asked.

Harold straightened his tie. "Imagine this—the entire town eating together in one sukkah. A combined Siegel House and Perfection on a Platter dinner event! Fun, right?"

"Hmmm . . . , " I thought out loud.

I could just imagine that. A huge celebration, with food from both Siegel House and Perfection on a Platter. Zadie is always saying that the point of Sukkot is having guests and making them feel welcome. How cool would it be to have a Sukkot dinner with everyone in town *at the same time*?

People wouldn't have to choose between our restaurants. It would be perfect for both our families. We could bring the Starlight Soup. The whole night could be wonder—

Suddenly, a terrible smell wafted into my nostrils.

I looked over at Harold.

He was opening his lunch box. Something inside reeked!

"Uhhh—what do you have for lunch?" I asked, trying not to gag.

Harold opened a plastic container.

"It's pickled herring," he said, grinning. "My family has been working on this for weeks. It's part of our Sukkot special."

I wrinkled my nose.

Pickled herring is probably my least favorite food on the planet. It smells nasty—like slimy fish covered in salt. Plus it looks like slugs in a jar.

"Ohhh . . . ummm looks great," I lied.

Harold smiled. "I know, right! So, what do you think about my idea?"

Chapter Seven
Grosser than Gross

I gulped.

I looked at the pickled herring and then back at Harold's face.

Honestly, I didn't know what to say. I like Harold. I really do. He's the only other kid in my class who reads cookbooks just for fun. And I didn't want to hurt his feelings or anything. But . . .

I took another tiny sniff.

Ugh!

The odor of the pickled herring flooded my nostrils. It made me shudder.

Suddenly, the combined Sukkot event didn't seem so fun anymore. There was no way we could serve our guests both the Starlight Soup and that nasty pickled herring.

"Harold, I . . ."

But he didn't let me finish. "I knew you'd love it! So, let's see—how about your restaurant brings the soup, the main dish, and the dessert? And my restaurant can do the salads, side dishes, and a big veggie platter!"

"But Harold . . ."

"Ohhh," he sighed. "Okay, you guys bring the side dishes. We'll do the dessert."

I crossed my arms. "No, Harold, we can't."

"What? Why?"

"I ummm . . . well it's just . . ."

Harold narrowed his eyes. "What?"

I took a deep breath.

"I just . . . we don't normally do dinners with other restaurants," I said.

"Come on, Saralee," said Harold, giving me a hopeful smile. "Imagine how special it would be for the whole town to eat together? It would be the best Sukkot ever."

But my mind was made up. We have really high culinary standards at Siegel House Restaurant. And what about my super-nose? I couldn't have people think that I gave the pickled herring my sniff of approval!

"I'm sorry, Harold," I said softly. "The answer is no."

Harold barely spoke to me for the rest of the day. Usually, we sit next to each other during art class. But today, Harold sat with Jacob Brodsky.

"All right, class," said Mr. Bloom, the art teacher. "It's creativity day. Feel free to work on your own project."

Sometimes, on creativity day, Harold and I make up an imaginary restaurant together and draw menu covers to go with it. We've already done Lava Burger (a restaurant on a volcano) and Submarine Sub Shop.

Only, when I looked across the room, Harold was already talking to Jacob. I guess he didn't want to make a menu cover today.

My stomach felt like a twisty pretzel.

I had so many fun restaurant ideas that I wanted to tell Harold about. A fake jewelry store, where the jewels are fancy candies. A tree house restaurant. Oh—and my newest idea—a dinosaur cafe (with robotic dinosaurs roaring every couple of minutes).

But obviously, Harold didn't want to hang out with me. So I grabbed some plain white paper from the shelf instead. I could make some flyers for tonight's Sukkot dinner. I mean, I didn't have anything else to work on.

Bring Starlight into the Sukkah, I wrote in loopy handwriting. *Enjoy our Starlight Soup.*

I looked up at Harold again. He was drawing something with Jacob. They were both smiling.

Fine, I thought, looking back down at my paper.

It wasn't my fault that Perfection on a Platter made gross food. Seriously, there was nothing I could do about that.

And plus, my Starlight Soup was definitely going to blow everyone's socks off. We didn't need a joint dinner with P.O.P. this year.

Chapter Eight
Perfection on a Platter

After school, Josh and I hung the flyers *every-where*—street lamps, mailboxes, even the trash cans.

People were already starting to talk about Starlight Soup. Word was spreading so quickly!

On our way home, Josh sat down on a bench and opened his doctor's bag. He took out his magnifying glass. "Hey, Saralee, look at my tongue."

"What? Why?" I asked.

Josh licked his lips. "I can *still* taste that yummy soup. Is my tongue red?"

I took the magnifying glass and studied Josh's tongue. It had little pink bumps, just like it always did.

"Looks fine to me."

But Josh was right—that Starlight Soup sure was strong. I could taste it too. And the taste seemed to be getting stronger. Maybe I needed to brush my teeth again?

I was just about to say so, when a stinky odor brushed my nostrils.

I cringed.

The whole neighborhood suddenly smelled like . . . like pickled herring! I pinched my nose and looked up at the street sign.

In all my excitement, I hadn't noticed my surroundings. We were just around the corner from the smelliest place on earth—Perfection on a Platter.

"Gross," I mumbled.

The pickled herring stunk up the whole street!

Harold Horowitz and his family were obviously getting ready for their Sukkot dinner tonight.

Thank goodness I hadn't agreed to a joint event.

Although . . .

A little teeny, tiny part of me wanted to know what they were doing over there. It's not that I wanted to *spy* on Harold or anything.

I was just curious. Very, very, very curious.

There's nothing wrong with a little curiosity . . . right?

"Hey, Josh," I said. "Let's do one more thing before we go home. I want to check out the competition."

Perfection on a Platter had big red letters above the front door. As we got closer, the smell of pickled herring grew overwhelming. My nose receptacles felt like they were going to explode.

But we didn't turn back.

Quietly, Josh and I tiptoed to the back of

the restaurant. From our hiding spot, we had a full view of the P.O.P. sukkah. And boy, it was completely different from ours!

Instead of a wooden frame, the Horowitzes had shiny metal. Tapestries with big geometric designs hung from the walls.

In the center of the sukkah was a large buffet table filled with fancy platters. I could smell lots of different dips—guacamole, spinach and artichoke, hummus, and French onion. Of course, the yucky pickled herring was right in the middle.

"Ewww," I mumbled under my breath.

I watched as the Horowitzes hurried to get things ready. The seating hostess robot zoomed all over the sukkah. It wore a frilly apron and was setting the tables at lightning speed.

Harold was in the corner, setting up a little table for the etrog. He surrounded the etrog with flowers and rocks.

"Hey, Mom," Harold called, backing up to admire his work. "Come look at my—"

I cringed as Harold bumped straight into the

seating hostess robot. The robot zoomed out of control, crashing into the etrog table.

"Uh-oh," I whispered.

The beautiful fruit fell to the floor and the robot rolled right over it!

SQUISH!

The etrog was completely ruined.

"What in the world," screeched Mrs. Horowitz.

Her hair was twisted back in a tight bun. She had a bony face, and she wore a crisp suit the color of dark chocolate.

"I'm sorry, Mom," mumbled Harold, looking at the ruined etrog.

"Don't you know how important this holiday is?" yelled Mrs. Horowitz. "Come on, Harold! We need to get all the details right. If we don't get more customers during this holiday . . . we're as good as done."

I lowered my eyes. *Done?* What did that mean? *Was Harold's restaurant in trouble?*

Harold's shoulders sagged.

Suddenly, my insides felt all crazy—like one of those baking soda and vinegar volcanoes. Harold looked miserable. I hated seeing him like that.

Maybe I should've said yes to Harold's idea . . . maybe a joint dinner wasn't such a bad—

The scent of pickled herring wafted toward me.

I squeezed my nose shut. *Yuck!*

Okay . . . never mind. I'd definitely made the right decision. But I just wished that Harold didn't look so sad. Obviously, coming here was a mistake.

I grabbed Josh's hand. "Let's go home."

Chapter Nine
Starlight Soup

That afternoon, my entire family scrambled around with last-minute preparations.

Josh and I made a big paper chain. Bubbie made sukkah decorations out of dried noodles. Aunt Bean folded and refolded the napkins until they were shaped like perfect little leaves. And Uncle Sam stood on a tall ladder, finishing a huge sculpture out of gourds.

"Hey, guys," he called, flailing his arms. "Look at my—"

CRASH!

The top gourd fell to the ground. It burst open, and the seeds splattered everywhere.

Immediately, Aunt Bean dropped the napkin in her hands and dashed for the broom and dustpan.

"I got it!" she called. "Don't move an inch."

Of course, during this whole fiasco, my aunt Lotte just lounged around reading a magazine. Aunt Lotte is the Siegel House waitress. She usually spends her days shouting orders into the kitchen real loud and taking breaks every seven minutes.

Soon the sun sank deep into the sky. A chilly breeze shook the branches on the sukkah's roof, and I wrapped my scarf snug against my neck.

"You ready to make the soup?" Zadie asked, calling me over to the outdoor kitchen.

Seven large pots filled with water sat on the counter.

"You think this'll be enough?" asked Zadie. "I bet the whole town will show up tonight."

I beamed. "Really? The whole town?"

Zadie nodded. "It's gonna be a busy night. People just can't resist a creative new dish."

Zadie beckoned me forward and tied a dish

towel around my eyes. It was time to go into over-smell.

I got all quiet and let my nose focus. Again, I smelled my way into the night sky. I sniffed past the sharp autumn air and the cotton candy clouds. I sniffed higher and higher until my nose could smell the big, wide universe.

Space still smelled of smoke and ashes, hot metal, and dust.

And I sniffed and sniffed and sniffed until I found my way back to the stars. I breathed in the delicious scent. The stars still smelled of all my favorite foods—kosher dill pickles, potato pancakes, and cheesy blintzes with strawberry jam.

Honestly, I could've just sat there forever, surrounded by the smell of starlight.

But then I imagined the starlight flavor flying into the soup pot. The air around me began to heat up. I could feel steam swirling around me, and I lifted the dishcloth from my eyes.

"Wow," Zadie whispered.

The pots of water were bubbling and steaming. Starlight radiated from the soup. The light filled every nook and cranny of our sukkah.

My whole family stopped their work to stare. Our sukkah was like the night sky—an array of silver stars twinkling brightly. The soup pots shone brighter than any light bulb. They were filled with pure light straight from the sky.

I could hear voices somewhere in the distance.

The guests were coming!

Zadie handed me the etrog. "Can you put this in the sukkah? Sukkot's not Sukkot without an etrog. It smells like a little slice of heaven."

I swallowed, suddenly thinking of Harold at Perfection on a Platter. I wondered what was going on over there.

Did they find a new etrog?

Were they getting enough guests?

I shook my head.

I didn't have time to think about Harold right now. We were about to give our guests the best Sukkot they'd ever had.

"Here we go," I said, walking into the sukkah. "Time for Starlight Soup."

Zadie was right.

The entire town was out there, waiting excitedly for their dinner. The line zigzagged down the block and around the corner. The guests were bundled in knitted hats, scarves, and mittens. Their faces were pink from the wind.

Of course, Siegel House Restaurant ran like clockwork. Bubbie welcomed the guests and led them to their seats.

"This way, Pookie Wookie," she called. "A special table just for you."

Zadie put on his puffy white chef hat. Aunt Bean made sure the tables were spick-and-span. Josh walked around with the etrog, giving everyone a chance to smell it. And Uncle Sam started chopping the vegetables for the crunchy pomegranate salad. He made a mound of cabbage on the cutting board so high, I could barely see his face.

Even Aunt Lotte helped. She carried the trays of food to the tables (even if she did roll her eyes just a little).

It was my job to serve the Starlight Soup.

All evening long, I carried bowl after bowl to the customers. The guests *oohed* and *ahhed*. They couldn't believe their taste buds.

"Oh man! It's super creamy broccoli cheddar," cried Jacob Brodsky.

"It's my favorite, egg drop soup," gasped Rachel Rubin. "Unbelievable!"

"How did you make this?" asked Mr. Green, the shopkeeper. "How'd you get my family's recipe for wild rice soup?"

One after another, our guests dined in our starlight sukkah. I loved hearing everyone's favorite soup flavor!

Creamy celery.

Red lentil.

Chicken dumpling.

Butternut squash.

Black bean.

Someone even tasted cream of dill pickle.

broccoli
egg
celery
dumpling
squash
beans
pickle

"This is the best Sukkot ever," I heard someone say.

From across the sukkah, Zadie winked at me.

I felt all warm and fuzzy inside—like when you bite into a roll with melted butter.

There were only smiles tonight at Siegel House Restaurant. Smiles and starlight—two of my favorite things.

Chapter Ten
Everyone in Town

The evening went by in a blur of people and soup bowls. When the last customer left for the night, I yawned and stretched out my arms. My whole body was tired and sore, but in a good way.

I looked around the sukkah. My family was busy closing everything down. Aunt Bean wore her rubber gloves and scrubbed all the surfaces. Uncle Sam ate a huge plate of leftovers. And Josh was sitting at one of the tables, trying to keep his eyes open. His head kept drooping every few seconds.

The Starlight Soup pots were completely empty. The customers had eaten every last drop.

I licked my lips.

Hmmm . . .

I could *still* taste that Golden Carrot flavor. Even after all this time—the taste hadn't gone away.

"Hey, guys," I said. "Do you still taste the Starlight Soup? Powerful stuff, right?"

"You betcha," Zadie called back. "Might be the strongest flavor I've ever tasted."

"Agreed," said Aunt Lotte. She leaned back in her chair and put her feet on the table.

Aunt Bean glared at her.

I started clearing the dirty napkins, letting my thoughts ramble. I wondered when the taste would finally fade. Maybe later tonight? Maybe tomorrow? It sure was lasting a long time.

When the sukkah was clean and sparkly, we all stumbled straight to bed. I wrapped myself in the covers and closed my eyes. I couldn't wait to do this all again tomorrow night! A whole week of beautiful Sukkot dinners—what could be better?

The last thing I remembered before falling asleep was the taste of Starlight Soup still on my tongue.

It happened in the middle of the night. I sat up in bed, my heart beating fast. Something was wrong. Really, really wrong.

I stuck out my tongue.

What was happening?

The taste on my tongue had grown even stronger. I could scarcely breathe. The whole world felt like one big Golden Carrot Soup. It didn't taste good anymore. It was too strong. Too overwhelming.

I needed water, and I needed it now!

Fast as I could, I ran downstairs and opened the kitchen door.

To my surprise, my whole family was already there. They were all in their pajamas, guzzling big cups of water.

"It's just so strong," muttered Aunt Bean. "I can't get this taste out."

She held her super-strength electric toothbrush in her hands. "Even brushing didn't work."

"Same with me," said Uncle Sam.

He opened a bunch of peppermint candies and popped them into his mouth all at the same time.

Josh was trying to look at his tongue with a tiny mirror.

"Yuck," he cried.

Aunt Lotte stomped around the kitchen in a bad mood.

"You've got to be kidding me," she huffed. "How am I supposed to have my midnight chocolate if all I can taste is SOUP!"

She tossed her chocolate bar away and frowned.

Even Bubbie looked concerned.

57

"It's too many noodles, Pookie Wookie. Way too much."

I swallowed.

Uh-oh.

No one could *stop* tasting Starlight Soup. If anything, the flavor was just growing more powerful.

How could this have happened?

I filled up a water cup and drank as fast as I could. But it didn't help at all. The taste just stayed in my mouth, covering my tongue like a damp washcloth.

"Uchhh," I groaned.

"Golly, this isn't good," Zadie muttered. "This isn't good at all."

I squeezed my eyes shut, wishing this was all just a dream.

Zadie was right—there was something wrong with the Starlight Soup. And we had just given a bowl to everyone in town!

Chapter Eleven
Carrots, Carrots, CARROTS

None of us could sleep for the rest of the night.

My tongue was so uncomfortable. All I wanted to do was taste something different. Anything different. I was so tired of Golden Carrot Soup, I thought I might be sick.

The next morning, no one wanted to get out of bed.

"I'm not feeling so well," said Zadie before I left for school. "Hopefully, I'll get better before the restaurant opens tonight. I just . . . I can't get that taste out of my mouth. It's overwhelming."

My eyes filled with tears. This was not what I had in mind when I set out to make Starlight Soup.

Suddenly, the doorbell rang. *Ding-Dong.*

"Can you get it, Saralee?" whispered Zadie.

I nodded and walked to the front entrance. My whole body felt heavy, like those big bags of flour at the grocery store.

Slowly, I opened the door.

I blinked a couple of times.

"Harold?" I asked. "Harold, what are you doing here?"

Harold Horowitz stood on my front steps. Just like every day, his red hair was gelled into a spike on the top of his head.

"I uhhh," he mumbled. "You know, I ummm wanted to see if you . . ."

Harold looked down at his toes.

"No one came to Perfection on a Platter last night," he explained. "We just sat outside for hours . . . waiting. But no one showed up."

I gulped.

"Was your family upset?" I asked.

Harold's cheeks turned pink. "Yeah. We had to throw a lot of food away. Well, not the pickled herring. That stuff lasts forever. But a lot of other stuff."

We stood in silence for a moment. Honestly, it was awkward. I tried to think of something to say, but all I could focus on was carrots, carrots, CARROTS!

"So why are you here?" I finally asked.

Harold shifted his feet.

"Well, I thought about it," he said. "And I want to try the soup. The whole town has been talking about it."

"*You* want to try Starlight Soup?"

"Yep," said Harold. "Last night was really rough. I need something yummy to cheer me up. Wanna have lunch together at school? I'll bring some stuff from my restaurant too. It could be fun—like a picnic!"

For a moment, I just stood there, staring at him.

There was no way I could give Harold Starlight Soup. He'd be trapped like the rest of us—tasting his favorite soup flavor for all of eternity.

I'm nice enough to know that friends don't give other friends dangerous soup.

"I'm sorry, Harold," I said. "But I can't."

Chapter Twelve
A Real Bummer

"What do you mean? Why?" asked Harold.

"It's a long story," I said. "Let's just say that Starlight Soup turned out to be a real bummer."

Harold crossed his arms.

Then he narrowed his eyes at me. "You're just making that up. I'm not gullible, you know."

"Harold, I promise you I'm telling the truth. I thought Starlight Soup was amazing. But then last night the craziest thing happened. I couldn't stop tasting—"

Harold didn't let me finish. "Just admit it. I'm your competition. You're afraid we're going to copy the soup and steal your guests."

"No, that's not—"

Harold's face was completely red now. "You know, first you shot down all of my Sukkot ideas. Then you made sure that everyone came here for dinner last night. And now, you won't even let me *try* the soup?"

"Harold, I'm just trying to protect you."

"Protect me?" Harold yelled. "Seriously? No, you're just being a terrible friend."

"Just let me explain," I started. "The Starlight Soup isn't safe—"

But Harold was having none of it.

"I'm out of here," he said, straightening his tie. "And don't bother sitting with me at lunch."

I watched as Harold stomped down the sidewalk.

My nose twitched.

This situation was getting out of control. Harold was super mad at me. And it wouldn't be long before all the customers realized that there was something wrong with their tongues.

By the end of the day, the whole TOWN was going to be upset with me.

Suddenly, I felt something pressing into my back. I whirled around and found Josh standing behind me. He held a stethoscope and was trying to listen to my breathing.

"You hurt, Saralee?" he asked. "You're breathing really fast."

Hurt?

Of course I was hurt. This whole holiday was turning into one big fiasco.

"Oh, Josh," I sighed. "We're in deep, *deep* trouble."

Josh opened his doctor's bag. He took out a small bottle of aloe vera and rubbed some of the gel onto the back of my hand.

Aloe vera is supposed to numb the pain. Rub some of that stuff onto a sunburn and you can't feel it anymore.

But I didn't have the heart to tell Josh the truth—I wasn't hurting on the outside. I was hurting on the inside.

Aloe vera wasn't going to help.

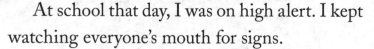

At school that day, I was on high alert. I kept watching everyone's mouth for signs.

Did they know yet?

Were they suspicious?

During lunch, the entire fifth grade gathered in the school's sukkah. Before we ate, Mr. Rosen, the principal, had each of us shake the *lulav* and etrog. The lulav is made up of branches from three plants. And it makes a nice swishy sound when you shake it.

When it was Harold's turn to hold the lulav and etrog, his ears turned bright red. He was probably thinking about his own etrog disaster.

I wanted to say something to him, but I wasn't sure what. So I ended up just staying quiet.

"Hey, Saralee," called Jacob Brodsky from across the sukkah. "It's amazing—I can still taste the Starlight Soup. How long do you think the flavor will last?"

I fidgeted with my jacket buttons.

"I uhhh . . . I don't know," I said back.

Only I *did* know. Jacob would taste his favorite soup forever if I couldn't find the cure.

Chapter Thirteen
Take Back Your Tongue

After school, things went from bad to worse. No one wanted to set up the sukkah for dinner tonight. Aunt Bean swept the same corner over and over again. Uncle Sam tried to chop some veggies but kept putting down his knife.

"Can't do it," he huffed, rubbing his bald spot. "I just can't."

Aunt Lotte refused to get out of bed. And Josh just sat in the corner, examining the tongues of all of his stuffed animals with a Popsicle stick from his doctor's bag.

Even Zadie looked out of sorts. He kept setting down his wooden spoon to gulp some water. Poor Bubbie sat at a table with her wire and dried noodles, but she couldn't create a single decoration.

"No more noodles," she sighed, getting up from her spot.

Around dinnertime, Mr. Green, the shop-keeper, came back to the sukkah. He held a huge water canteen in his hands.

"Oh, thank goodness," he said. "You've got to help me."

My whole family looked up.

"Help you?" squeaked Aunt Bean.

Mr. Green ran a hand through his hair. "It's my tongue. Something's wrong. I can't stop tasting the Starlight Soup. It's just over-whelming. Please tell me there's something you can do."

I couldn't help it—my hands began to shake.

Making Starlight Soup was MY idea. Zadie had trusted me to give the guests something fresh and new. And now . . . things were getting crazy.

Zadie patted Mr. Green on the back.

"I am so sorry," he said sadly. "We . . . we don't know how to fix it yet."

Mr. Green frowned. "But you guys made the soup. Are you saying this is . . . *permanent*?"

Zadie shook his head.

"Listen, we're working on it," he said. "We'll let you know when we figure out the cure for the Starlight Soup. Until then, go home and get some rest."

Mr. Green frowned and headed out the door.

But the complaints didn't stop there. All evening long, customer after customer came back to Siegel House. Each of them had the same problem—they couldn't taste *anything* but the Starlight Soup.

They didn't want to order anything for dinner. All they wanted was for their tongues to go back to normal.

That night, I looked around our empty sukkah. It didn't feel warm and cozy anymore. The tables were empty. The kitchen was bare.

I squeezed my super-nose between my fingers.

I had to fix this. I just had to. After all, my nose is like an encyclopedia of flavors and scents.

"Come on, nose," I whispered. "Tell me what to do. I need to fix this holiday. Please, please, PLEASE—tell me how to cure Starlight Soup."

At school the next day, no one was acting like themselves. Everyone looked dazed and carried around big water bottles.

Even my teacher, Mrs. Stearns, seemed out of sorts. She kept having to sit down at her desk and put her head down.

"I'm sorry," she said during math class. "I'm really not feeling well. My tongue—it's just . . ."

"Tasting like soup?" filled in Rachel Rubin.

Everyone turned around to look at me.

My cheeks flared.

Even Harold was looking. I wondered if he was still mad at me, considering that I had saved him from the terrible Starlight Soup tongue.

During lunch, the school sukkah was almost silent. All the kids were just staring at their lunches without touching them.

Honestly, I didn't have an appetite either. I couldn't even think about eating with the taste of Golden Carrot Soup getting stronger in my mouth.

Only one person chomped on a sandwich—Harold Horowitz.

I sat down next to him and took a gulp from my water bottle.

"See," I said to him. "Aren't you glad I didn't let you have any of that Starlight Soup?"

Hey, this whole situation was a mess—but at least I can say I did the right thing by Harold Horowitz.

Harold crossed his arms.

"I don't want to talk to you, Saralee," he said.

Seriously? What now? I didn't understand this at all!

Harold should be grateful. I *could* have given him that soup and let him suffer with the rest of us. But obviously, I didn't do that. Obviously, I'm a good friend.

"I don't get it," I said. "Why are you so mad?"

Harold looked down at the table.

"Sheesh, Saralee," he mumbled. "All you ever think about is yourself. No one came to my restaurant the first night of Sukkot because they were all excited about Starlight Soup. And now that they've had it—no one wants to eat anything *at all*. We've had zero guests so far."

I scratched my cheek.

"Harold, I didn't mean for this to happen," I said. "Really, I didn't."

Harold opened his lunch box and took out a stack of papers.

"I know you didn't," he said. "But I told you—I was excited to have guests in the sukkah. And my family was counting on some serious sales. You ruined all that. So now we're changing our plan."

He began handing out papers to everyone.

"What's that?" I asked.

Hesitantly, Harold passed a paper to me. I stared at it for a moment, scarcely believing my eyes.

"How did you . . . what in the world?" I stuttered.

The paper had P.O.P's logo on the top.

TAKE BACK YOUR TONGUE, it said.

"Thank goodness," cried Jacob Brodsky. "I can't stand this anymore. What would we do without you, Harold?"

I couldn't believe this.

How did Harold figure out the cure? He hadn't even tried the soup!

Chapter Fourteen
Barely Working

Everyone was talking about the Take-Back-Your-Tongue event for the rest of the day. After school, I ran to the kindergarten room as fast as I could. I had to tell Josh about this immediately.

Only he already knew about it.

He took one of the flyers out of his doctor's bag and handed it to me.

"Look!" he said. "They fixed it."

Suddenly, out of the corner of my eye, I saw a

streak of red hair. I looked up. Harold Horowitz was rushing down the hallway.

"Come on," I whispered, taking Josh's hand. "We've got to see what they're planning."

I just had to know how the Horowitzes figured out the cure. I mean, *I'm* the one with the super-nose. How did Harold figure this out?

We followed Harold down the hallway and out the door. We were careful to keep our distance so he wouldn't see us.

Outside, I tried to take a deep sniff with my super-nose.

The trees were the color of clementines and red bell peppers. Acorns lay scattered across the sidewalk. And the rain had made the grass shoot up like weeds.

The smells of autumn *should* have been strong and powerful. My nose receptacles *should* have been bursting with flavor.

But my nose was filled with only one scent— Golden Carrot Soup.

Oh no.

Oh NO NO NO NO!

All I could smell was Starlight Soup. The magic was growing so strong, even my super-nose was affected.

Up ahead, Harold headed toward Main Street. I had to get myself together. I couldn't worry about the terrible taste on my tongue or my faulty nose. I just had to know what Harold was planning for tonight.

I could try to fix my nose later.

Harold ducked into the grocery store. Josh and I were close behind.

I spotted Harold in the vegetable section. He was filling his cart with chili peppers.

Chili peppers?

What did they have to do with Starlight Soup? And why was Harold buying so many of them?

Mr. Green walked into the vegetable section.

"Oh, excuse me," called Harold.

I inched closer so I could hear.

"I need to buy ice. Lots and lots of ice," said Harold. "But your ice machine is empty. . . ."

Ice? I thought.

Chili peppers and ice? What a strange combination.

Mr. Green shook his head sadly.

"All gone," he said. "Everyone's been buying tons of ice to chew on today. No one can get that disastrous soup flavor out of their mouth. The ice helps for a little bit—but then the taste comes right back."

I felt like someone had just dropped heavy stones into my stomach.

Mr. Green had called the soup *disastrous*.

Harold bit his fingernails.

"Are you sure you don't have more?" he asked. "I need a ton of it for tonight. Way more than what we have at my restaurant."

Mr. Green nodded. "I'm sure. We're totally out. By the way, I'll be at your event tonight. Thank goodness you guys figured out the cure."

I scratched my forehead.

Ice and chili peppers? What could Harold do with that?

I closed my eyes and tried to focus my super-nose. It was getting really hard, considering that my nose receptacles were filled with the smell of Golden Carrot Soup.

But I tried my best to imagine the flavor factory inside my nostrils. I imagined little nose scientists hurrying around, experimenting with flavors.

Ice and chili peppers.
Ice and chili peppers.
Ice and . . .

"Oh, my goodness," I whispered.

I had to steady myself against the shelf of potato chips.

I knew exactly what Harold was planning. And it wasn't a cure at all. See, when I put chili peppers in my stir fry, it burns my tongue. And when I chew on ice, it makes my tongue feel frozen. Put them together and—

The Horowitzes were going to numb people's tongues!

Chapter Fifteen
The Rest of Eternity

I looked up at Harold. He was still putting more chili peppers into his cart.

"I'm bored," whispered Josh. "I wanna go home."

He opened his doctor's bag and took out a pack of Band-Aids. He started sticking them all over his arms.

But I couldn't move a muscle.

Tongue numbing . . .

I never would have thought of that. It wasn't a

real cure, or anything. But at this point, I'd rather taste *nothing* than this awful Starlight Soup.

My chest tightened.

A terrible thought crossed my mind.

What if there wasn't a *real* cure? What if Harold had come up with the best possible solution?

I could just imagine it now—the whole town numbing their tongues for the rest of eternity. We'd all just walk around without tasting or smelling anything.

Our lives would be bland and boring.

And my super-nose would . . . it would be gone forever.

Suddenly, the taste of Starlight Soup felt stronger than ever. The flavor was so powerful, it almost tasted *burnt*.

I cringed.

There's nothing worse than burnt carrots cemented to the bottom of the soup pot.

I couldn't stand this anymore! I needed one of Harold's ice-and-chili-pepper mixtures. I needed to numb my tongue before I went crazy.

Only . . .

I watched as Harold pushed his cart over to the ice machine. He kept opening and closing it, frowning.

Harold didn't have all of the ingredients. He still needed more ice.

Taking a deep breath, I thought about what Harold had said during lunch. Perfection on a Platter hadn't had a single guest this entire holiday. They hadn't gotten a chance to celebrate Sukkot this year. And it was pretty much all because of Starlight Soup.

I bit my lip.

Maybe there was something I could do to help?

Back at home, the whole house was silent. No one seemed to notice as I wheeled our big red wagon into the kitchen. The ice machine was completely full. So I scooped the ice cubes into the wagon bit by bit.

The wagon was almost filled when Zadie walked by.

"What's going on?" he asked.

"It's uhhh . . . it's for Perfection on a Platter," I explained. "They're doing an event tonight called Take Back Your Tongue. But they need more ice. I thought I'd bring them some."

"Take Back Your Tongue?"

I nodded. "They're going to numb everyone's tongue. No one will be able to taste anything. You know . . . because of Starlight Soup."

Zadie pressed his lips together. "But Saralee, that's just a temporary fix. Don't you think your super-nose can come up with a real cure?"

My shoulders drooped.

"No," I said, my voice breaking. "My super-nose is broken. I can't sniff a single thing. And Harold's idea is better than nothing. Plus, he hasn't had a single Sukkot guest—and it's all my fault. I should help him."

Zadie nodded slowly.

I started to pull the wagon down the hall, but Zadie stopped me.

"Hey, Saralee," he said, squeezing my arm.

"Yeah?"

"You're doing the right thing. And when you're ready—I bet your super-nose will find the *real* cure."

My eyes filled with tears. "How can you be so sure?"

"I just have that feeling," he said. "From my experience, your super-nose can do *anything*. Just wait and see."

Chapter Sixteen
An Unexpected Smell

The wagon must've weighed a million gazillion pounds. I pulled it down the sidewalk, my heart pounding like an electric mixer at the highest speed.

By the time I got to Perfection on a Platter, I was shaking with nerves.

The last thing I wanted to do was face Harold and his family. But they *needed* this event tonight. And the townspeople needed a break from tasting soup. I had to help.

Slowly, I opened the door to Perfection on a Platter.

The dining room was empty. So I inched my way toward the kitchen, rolling the wagon behind me.

Thump-thump-thump, went the wheels.

I could hear voices. Lots and lots of voices.

Quietly, I peeked into the kitchen.

All the Horowitzes were there. Tonight, they wore sleek black suits and matching aprons. I could already see them blending the chili peppers into a paste.

I sniffed, wanting to smell out my surroundings. But no smells came to my nose.

Well, no smells except for a waft of pickled herring. A platter of that disgusting, slimy fish lay on the countertop.

Ugh, gross, I thought. *Harold's pickled herring is so nasty, even Starlight Soup can't block it out.*

"Saralee?" said a voice. "What are you doing here?"

I jumped.

Harold was looking right at me. There was no turning back now. Soon the rest of the Horowitzes looked up as well. My fingers and toes turned to icicles.

"My, my, my—it's Saralee Siegel," said Mrs. Horowitz. "What a surprise. Are you *spying* on us?"

My face turned red.

"No, no," I stammered.

I pulled the wagon full of ice from behind me and turned to Harold. "I ummm . . . I saw you at the grocery store earlier. I heard you needed this."

Harold moved closer. He stared at the ice and then back at me.

"But . . . ," he started. "Why are you . . . why are you helping us?"

I fidgeted in my spot. "You should get to host a Sukkot event too. . . . I wanted to help."

One of Harold's uncles plucked a piece of pickled herring from the countertop and tossed it into his mouth. He chewed it noisily.

I cringed as the smell of pickled herring grew stronger in my nose. Gosh, that stuff smelled foul.

"Well . . . ummm thanks," said Harold, bending down to take a handful of ice.

I wondered if he was still mad at me.

I really hoped he wasn't.

I wanted to draw menu covers with him again. I wanted to sit next to him at lunch and peruse cookbooks together during free time.

I just . . . missed him.

I know our restaurants compete for sales, but Harold is my best friend. And I really hoped this Starlight Soup business didn't mess that all up.

Across the room, Harold's uncle grabbed a second piece of herring. I wrinkled my nose as the stench of fish floated into my nostrils.

The smell was pure torture!

The herring smelled like a trash can full of . . .

Wait a minute!

I froze.

Had I really just smelled the pickled herring?

I sniffed a little harder.

Yes, I could actually smell it!

The pickled herring reeked of slimy fish covered in salt. I could smell it so clearly.

How was this possible?

For hours now, my nose was completely blocked with the smell of Starlight Soup. Why could I only smell the PICKLED HERRING?

Chapter Seventeen
Together

This didn't make any sense! I moved closer to the platter of pickled herring. I leaned in and took a little sniff.

"Holy moly macaroni," I said out loud.

The smell was strong. Really, *really* strong!

Pickled herring was my least favorite food in the whole universe. Why did it—

I gasped.

My mind swirled around and around with thoughts.

"Ummm, Saralee?" asked Harold. "Why are you just standing there?"

I looked up at him in shock. Could it really be so simple?

"Hey, Harold, can I try one of those?" I asked, pointing to the platter of fish.

Starlight Soup tasted like everyone's *favorite* soup flavor. Could I cure my tongue by trying my *least favorite* flavor?

Harold turned back around. "What? What are you talking about?"

"I want to try your pickled herring."

Harold rubbed his chin. "What's going on, Saralee?"

"I think I may be onto something," I said.

One of Harold's uncles frowned. "Are you trying to copy our special pickling brine? Because if you are . . ."

"No, it's nothing like that," I cried.

But Harold's uncle looked suspiciously at me.

I looked over at Harold. "Please, *pleeeeeaaase* can I try a piece of pickled herring?"

He nodded. "It's okay, guys. She's not going to copy it."

All the Horowitzes watched as I reached forward. I almost gagged when I felt the wet and slimy texture. The smell made me feel sick. The herring reeked of vinegar.

I shuddered and lifted a piece to my mouth.

My whole body started to squirm. All I wanted to do was set the fish down and run from the room. But I had to do this!

Squeezing my eyes shut, I began to chew. I chewed and chewed and chewed until . . . something incredible happened.

The intense taste of Golden Carrot Soup began to fade away. My tongue was free! For the first time in a long while, my mind felt clear.

I licked my lips.

Hmmm . . .

The pickled herring was not like I thought it would be. I still didn't like it, but it didn't taste rotten or anything. It was salty, like the ocean.

My nose twitched. Smells were beginning to flood into my nostrils. I could smell every ingredient in the entire Perfection on a Platter kitchen. I could smell the veggie platters, the homemade pita, and the guacamole trays. Finally, my super-nose was back!

"What's going on?" asked Mrs. Horowitz.

I grinned.

"It's gone," I said. "The Starlight Soup taste is completely gone."

I knew what I needed to do. Perfection on a Platter *needed* this event tonight. Forget the numbing smoothies! It was time for them to host a *real* Sukkot dinner for everyone in town.

"No need to numb people's tongues," I said. "I

think I figured out the real cure for Starlight Soup."

Harold's eyes grew wide. "What do you mean? The cure is eating pickled herring?"

I shook my head.

"No. Not at all! Starlight Soup tastes like your *favorite* soup flavor. So the cure is trying your *least favorite* flavor."

"How do you know that?"

I gave him a sheepish look.

"Well," I explained. "I just tried a piece of your pickled herring. For my whole life, herring has been my least favorite food. It's just so slimy. But it cleared the soup flavor right up."

Harold's eyes grew wide.

"This is for real?" he asked.

"Seriously," I said. "It's up to you guys now. Cure everyone here at the Take-Back-Your-Tongue event. Put out every disgusting thing you can think of—you know, raw brussels sprouts, sardines, blue cheese. That sort of thing."

The Horowitzes looked stunned. And honestly, there was nothing more I could do.

I'd told Harold about the cure, and now it

was up to him to actually give it to the guests and save Sukkot.

I walked toward the door.

"Wait—" called Harold.

I turned back around.

Harold's face was all pink.

"I . . . well . . . why don't you get some gross stuff from your restaurant too," he said. "We might not have *everyone's* least favorite food here. We can do a joint dinner—both of our restaurants together."

I suddenly felt all light—like a fizzy soda bursting with bubbles.

"Really?" I asked, looking at Mrs. Horowitz.

She put her hands on her hips. "We're starting in one hour. *Don't* be late."

I was just about to run out the door when I turned around and gave Harold a hug.

"Thank you," I said.

Harold grinned. "No problem. This was just what I wanted—a dinner with both of our restaurants. Maybe this will turn out to be the best Sukkot yet?"

Chapter Eighteen
Yucky Platters

I ran home as fast as I could. My nose filled with the smells of a thousand things.

Gosh . . . I'd missed this.

I reveled in the scent of every fallen leaf, every flower growing in the cracks of the sidewalk.

I dashed through the front door. All of my relatives were lying on the couch, barely moving.

"I've found the cure," I declared. "And you won't believe what it is."

I explained what had happened at Perfection on a Platter.

"You're kidding me," said Aunt Lotte. "All I have to do is eat overcooked spinach . . . and this taste will go away?"

"Correct," I said, smiling.

Uncle Sam bolted off the couch. He ran to the kitchen and started rummaging through the cupboards. I could hear things falling onto the floor.

Only a few moments later, everyone sat eating their least favorite foods. Bubbie covered a plate full of noodles with hot sauce. Josh held his nose and shoved a  radish into his mouth. Zadie opened a can of anchovies. Even Aunt Bean was brave. She strode over to the refrigerator and took out an unwashed peach.

"This thing has been on the ground. It's covered in dirt . . . it's . . . it's . . ."

She took a bite and sighed.

"It's divine," she whispered. "Dirty . . . but divine."

When everyone's tongues had gone back to normal, I told them my next piece of news. We were doing a joint dinner at Perfection on a Platter.

"Are you serious?" asked Aunt Bean. "Every one's going to get their Starlight Soup cure there? Why don't we just invite everyone *here*?"

I shook my head.

"I sort of ruined their Sukkot plans," I explained. "They had all this stuff planned. And it got canceled because of Starlight Soup. They haven't had a single guest this entire holiday. I think we should let them host this event. We'll bring all of our gross food over there."

Aunt Bean was about to protest, but Zadie stood up and patted my back.

"It's a great idea," he said. "Let's fill up the wagon lickety-split."

My family sprang into action.

We scavenged the kitchen for the grossest ingredients possible. We found cottage cheese and greasy french fries, bitter brussels sprouts and raw mushrooms, stinky hard-boiled eggs and spongy tofu, plain mayonnaise, overripe melon, and cookies burnt to a crisp.

I smiled, breathing in all the nasty smells.

Uncle Sam heaved the wagon down the hallway. And that's when I smelled the etrog. The sunny, easy breezy etrog.

Zadie was right; the etrog *did* smell like a little piece of heaven. I'd missed this smell so much!

Hmmm . . .

I thought about Harold. He didn't have an etrog anymore.

Quietly, I scooped up the etrog and put it in my jacket pocket. Then I followed my family into the night.

Chapter Nineteen
Teeny Tiny Little Bit

When we got to Perfection on a Platter, Harold and his family were waiting for us.

"The Siegels. We meet again," said Mrs. Horowitz.

Zadie walked forward and stuck out his hand.

"It's a pleasure sharing this evening with you. Shall we lay out the disgusting platters?"

Mrs. Horowitz nodded. "Let's do it."

While both of our families got to work on

the food platters, Harold and I escaped into the P.O.P. sukkah with a plate of pickled herring and some water. There were *waaaaaay* too many cooks in the kitchen tonight. We definitely needed a break from all the shenanigans.

I took the etrog out of my pocket and handed it to him. "I figured you might need this for dinner tonight."

Harold's eyes grew wide. "I . . . uhhh . . . Saralee, thank you. We actually don't have an etrog anymore. It . . . ummm . . . it got squished. The pesky seating hostess robot rolled over it."

We both laughed.

I smiled and looked at my surroundings.

The P.O.P. sukkah was filled with square tables with checkered tablecloths. They had fancy glass centerpieces full of flowers. The whole thing was nice, I guess. But . . . I couldn't help but feel a little sad.

Nothing could compare to our starlit sukkah. It had truly been a spectacular sight. And without Starlight Soup, I'd never see a sukkah like that again.

Well . . . maybe there was *something* I could do.

Maybe I could make a teeny tiny little bit of Starlight Soup? And I wouldn't let anyone eat it! That would be fine, *right*?

I took a sip of water.

"Okay, don't be scared," I said. "But I'm going to make a little bit more Starlight Soup."

Harold gave me a look. "Isn't that stuff dangerous?"

I nodded. "Yeah, but it's NOT for eating. It's just . . . I want to see the beautiful starlight again. Even if we can't *taste* it. It will make your sukkah look magical, I promise."

Harold nodded slowly. "Just be careful."

"Okay, I know this is weird," I started. "But can you tie a towel around my head?"

He wrapped a P.O.P. dishcloth around my eyes and ears. The whole world turned dark and silent. And my super-nose took in the smells of the night.

I could smell all sorts of disgusting things coming from the kitchen—burnt toast, chopped liver, and overripe bananas. But I ignored those smells and let my nose soar through the night sky.

I'd never *ever* get tired of this.

My nose flew past the clouds and drifted into space. Everything out here smelled of smoke and ashes. I sniffed past the hot-metal sun and the dusty moon. I sniffed past *everything* until I reached the stars.

Suddenly, the water cup I held grew hot. I could feel it start to bubble and steam.

Harold gasped.

I lifted the dish towel from my eyes and stared at the incredible sight.

The tiny cup of Starlight Soup was enough to light the entire P.O.P. sukkah.

"This is incredible," whispered Harold. "It's too bad we can't eat it. Because it looks amazing."

He popped a piece of pickled herring into his mouth. He chewed it noisily, and I could already smell its salty scent.

"I know, right?" I said. "It's the most amazing soup in all—"

Suddenly, my super-nose began to tingle. An idea formed in my mind.

I looked down at the Starlight Soup. And then back at the plate of pickled herring.

What if...

Chapter Twenty
Golden Carrot

My thoughts began to bounce around like crazy.

Maybe there *was* a way to eat Starlight Soup safely?

Slowly, I reached for a piece of pickled herring. Could this actually work? I dropped it into the cup with a *splash*. As soon as the herring hit the broth, it started to shimmer and glow.

Harold wrinkled his eyebrows together, confused.

Hopefully, this would do the trick. By

adding my least favorite flavor, maybe I could make Starlight Soup safe to eat?

"Here goes," I said, taking a little sip.

"Stop, Saralee," cried Harold. "What are you doing?"

But it was too late.

Starlight Soup still tasted like Golden Carrot. But it was a bit different this time. It tasted a little saltier, a little more flavorful. . . .

I swallowed and pursed my lips.

The taste immediately disappeared—just like a normal sip of soup.

"Perfect," I cried, turning to Harold. "The guests are going to love this! Wanna try?"

"It's safe?" he asked.

I nodded. "If you add your least favorite flavor, the taste disappears just like normal."

Harold's face split into a grin. He ran into the kitchen to get some spicy horserad-ish. He squirted some into the cup and then lifted the soup to his lips.

"Yum," he cried. "Wow, this is incredible. It tastes just like my favorite soup of all time

—Golden Carrot! How did you do this?"

My eyes grew wide.

No way!

"Your favorite soup is *Golden Carrot*?" I exclaimed.

Harold nodded. "Oh yeah—this was the first recipe I ever made by myself. Like seriously . . . no adults or anything. I made the whole thing from scratch."

I opened my mouth.

And then closed it again.

"So what do *you* taste?" Harold asked. "What's your favorite soup?"

"I ummm . . . well, this is crazy," I said breathlessly. "But it's the same as yours— Golden Carrot Soup. It's been my favorite soup for years."

Harold smiled at me. "No kidding. We're soup twins."

Suddenly, my heart felt so full I thought it would burst.

Thank the stars, I had my friend back.

Chapter Twenty-One
Always Sniffing

The New and Improved Starlight Soup was a huge success. We all worked hard to keep the dinner running smoothly.

Both Bubbie and the seating hostess robot helped the customers find their seats.

Bubbie looked the robot up and down. It was wearing a fancy embroidered apron.

"I like your outfit, Pookie Wookie," Bubbie said.

"Thank you," said the seating hostess robot in its robotic voice. "I like your necklace."

Bubbie blushed, touching her chain made of macaroni. "Why thank you. I have an extra one if you would like it."

She took out a noodle necklace from her pocket and slipped it over the robot's head.

Meanwhile, all the uncles kept the platters filled with food. Zadie and Mrs. Horowitz traveled from table to table, checking on the customers. And Aunt Bean kept the buffet tidy and clean.

It was my job to ladle the Starlight Soup into bowls. And Harold helped everyone add their least favorite foods.

I watched as Mrs. Stearns dropped some raw broccoli into her glowing broth. She took a spoonful, and her face lit up into a smile.

Rachel Rubin had a bowl with uncooked mushrooms. And Jacob Brodsky poured a cup of tomato juice into his soup.

It was pretty cool to see everyone's face turn from disgust to joy in a single second. And it was nice that no one had to pick between Siegel House and Perfection on a Platter. We were all eating at the same place.

Later that night, I took a break and sat down at one of the P.O.P tables. Zadie came to sit beside me.

He wrapped his arm around my shoulder and pulled me close. He smelled just like he always did: peppermint with a hint of corned beef on rye.

We sat like that for a good long while, just watching our friends and neighbors eat bowl after bowl of the new and improved Starlight Soup. We sat there until the line thinned out and the air grew chilly.

"Ahhh," said Zadie, zipping up his jacket. "You know what? I think this may have been the most interesting Sukkot we've ever had. And I've never seen the guests look so happy."

I smiled and looked up through the roof of the sukkah.

It was a dazzling night. The moon shone brilliantly in the inky-black sky. And the stars seemed to glow brighter than ever before. It was as if they were shining just for us.

Later, I went to look for Harold.

"This dinner was amazing," I gushed. "Seriously, we should do a joint dinner again next Sukkot."

"Yes, definitely," Harold said with a smile. "And here—"

He held out the etrog. "Thanks for letting us use it tonight."

I held the etrog tightly in my hands, breathing in its delicious scent.

I looked around the sukkah. Almost all the guests had gone home. The seating hostess robot was making noodle art with Bubbie. And Aunt Lotte was snoozing in a chair.

"You know," I said to Harold. "It looks like things are pretty much under control around here. Wanna play the 'Find the Etrog' game?"

Harold pinched his hair spike. "Uhhh, sure. How do you play?"

I gave him back the etrog. "You hide the etrog anywhere around town. Seriously, think of the best hiding spot you can."

"Okay . . . ," said Harold.

"When you come back, I'll have fifteen minutes to sniff it out."

Harold grinned. "You're on! I'll beat you no problem."

I laughed out loud.

"Don't be so sure," I said. "I've never lost a game."

Without another word, Harold sprinted down the sidewalk with the etrog. He came back eight minutes later, huffing and puffing.

"You will never EVER find the etrog now!" he shouted.

I stood up and handed him my watch. "Oh, yeah? We'll see about that."

Harold clenched the watch between his fingers.

"Prove it," he said. "On your mark, get set, GO!"

I ran as fast as I could, my super-nose taking in the scents of the neighborhood. The air smelled of pine cones with a hint of sweet pumpkin pie. But I pushed those smells away, sniffing for that etrog. Sniffing for that easy, breezy afternoon with clear skies. I sniffed and sniffed and sniffed, until . . .

"Aha!" I cried out loud. "Gotcha."

I could smell the etrog clearly now. All I had to do was follow the trail.

The End

Saralee's Starlight Soup Recipe

Golden Carrot Soup

Makes approximately 12 cups

Before making this delicious soup, ask an adult for permission, and always have an adult help when you need to use a knife or the stove.

Ingredients

2 tablespoons olive oil
2 cups leeks, white part only, thinly sliced
2 ½ pounds carrots, peeled, trimmed, and roughly chopped
3 McIntosh apples, peeled and roughly chopped
4 cups vegetable stock
2 cups apple cider
1 teaspoon ground turmeric
½ teaspoon cinnamon
½ inch knob of fresh ginger, grated (about 2 teaspoons)
salt and pepper, to taste
1 cup coconut milk
1–2 tablespoons honey
For garnish: A little more coconut milk, a drizzle of honey, freshly ground pepper, and a cinnamon stick (all optional)

Directions

1. Heat olive oil in a large soup pot. Add the leeks, and sauté until softened.

2. Add the carrots, apples, stock, cider, turmeric, cinnamon, ginger, salt, and pepper; bring the mixture to a simmer. Cook until the carrots are soft, about 30–40 minutes.

3. Puree in batches in a blender, or use an immersion blender. Add the coconut milk and honey, to taste (depending on desired sweetness). If the soup is too thick, add water, stock, or more apple cider until desired consistency is reached.

4. To serve, swirl in more coconut milk, and add a drizzle of honey, freshly ground black pepper, and a cinnamon stick, if desired.

Recipe copyright © Chanie Apfelbaum, from her kosher cooking blog, www.busyinbrooklyn.com

Elana Rubinstein is the author of *Once Upon an Apple Cake*. She is an early childhood educator in Los Angeles, California.

Jennifer Naalchigar also illustrated *Once Upon an Apple Cake*. She has been drawing ever since she was old enough to hold a pencil. She lives in Hertfordshire, England.